PRINCESS POPPY'S PARTY

WRITTEN AND ILLUSTRATED BY

JANEY JONES

Peppermint press

Poppy woke up early.

"YIPPEE!" she shouted.

"It's my BIRTHDAY!"

Poppy jumped out of bed.

"Birthdays are great fun. I'll be a special Princess all day today!" she said.

Poppy looked around her bedroom, which was full of old toys, books and dressing-up clothes. *Hmmmm* she thought, *nothing for a Birthday Princess in here.*

"Well, I hope everyone has remembered my birthday," she said, with her hands on her hips.

Poppy put on her prettiest red dress, brushed her golden hair and fixed her poppy clips into her hair.

“I’m off to find my birthday things!” she decided.

Poppy dashed through to her Mummy’s room.

“Here I am, Mummy,” said Poppy.

“Oh, Poppy, I’m still sleepy,” said Mummy, from under the bedcovers.

“But, it’s my birth..” Poppy began.
“Go back to bed for half an hour,” mumbled Mummy.

“How could Mummy sleep late on my special day?” wondered Poppy, crossly.

Poppy went back to lie on her bed.
“This is boring,” decided the little birthday girl.

So, Poppy went next door to talk to Mrs Bumble, who *always* got up early.

Mrs Bumble had just chopped up some strawberries, and was now whisking eggs and flour.

"Mrs Bumble, it's my birth.."

"Poppy, can't you see I'm busy? Come back later," said Mrs Bumble, pointing to the door.

Oh no! Even Mrs Bumble doesn't care that it's my birthday, thought Poppy.

"Right, that's it!" she decided, "I'm going to see my Grandpa at his office. He would *never* forget my birthday."

Poppy knocked on the big, green office door.

“Come in!” boomed Grandpa.

Grandpa was hiding behind a large newspaper.
“Can’t talk, dear!” said Grandpa, “I’m stuck on my crossword!”

Poppy closed the door with a BANG!

“Not Grandpa too,” said Poppy.
“Anyway, his newspaper was upside down!”

SAFFRONTHIMBLE

Next, Poppy peeped through the window of Saffron Thimble's sewing shop. Saffron was busy stitching a beautiful red ballgown.

"Hi, Saffron, what a beautiful dress! Did you know it's.."

"Oh, Poppy, I've got to get on with this job. I'm making this for a girl I know who can't wait for anything. I don't have time to chat," said Saffron, kneeling on her shop floor.

Poppy went to find her best friend, Honey, in the Lavender Garden.

Honey was dressed up in her fairy outfit.

"Did *you* remember my birthday?" Poppy asked her best friend.

"Oh, Poppy, I didn't forget, but I haven't exactly remembered right now, if you see what I mean," said Honey, sounding confused.

Poor Poppy felt oh so sad. It was as if no one cared enough about her to remember her special day.

"I just don't understand it. Mummy always says I'm a special Princess on my birthday," she told Honey.

"Come with me Poppy, let's go to play in the courtyard," suggested Honey, looking at the big village clock.

As Poppy and Honey arrived, they heard beautiful music playing. Honey opened the gates to the courtyard.

"SURPRISE!"

Streamers, balloons and flower petals showered down on Poppy's head. "BANG!" went the party poppers.

"HAPPY BIRTHDAY!" shouted Poppy's family and friends.

N
W
E

"Oh WOW!" said Poppy.

"Thank you. You *have* remembered!"

“You’ve waited very patiently, darling,” said Mummy.

“Now you can open all your lovely presents!”

Mummy gave Poppy a bright red velvet box. Inside was a glittering necklace. Poppy put it on. “Sparkly!”

Mrs Bumble stepped forward with a strawberry sponge birthday cake.

Poppy blew out five glowing candles, then she tasted a slice.

"Deeeeelicious!"

Grandpa handed Poppy a beautiful tiara made of three poppies. Poppy tried it on her head. “Special!”

Then, Saffron Thimble came forward with a huge white box, covered with poppies, that had a red bow on top.

The label read :

Poppy opened the box, and pulled out the red Princess ball gown and red velvet shoes.

"Oh, Saffron, the dress was for *me*!" exclaimed Poppy. "I thought you said it was for a girl who can't wait for anything!"

Everyone started to laugh.

"Poppy," said Honey, "it's just after breakfast-time and you *have* been finding it hard to wait for your presents, haven't you?"

"Yes, you're right, I should have known something lovely was going to happen," giggled Poppy.

Honey then handed her friend a little glass bottle, with a red ribbon tied around it.

"It's petal perfume," Honey explained. "I made it myself."

"Oh, Honey, it smells lovely!" Poppy squealed as she dabbed the perfume behind her ears.

Poppy dashed away to try on her Princess dress.

When she came back in it, Grandpa said, “Poppy, you are the most beautiful Princess in the whole world!”

“Grandpa,” Poppy asked, “is every little girl a princess?”

“Yes, Poppy, every girl is a Princess, especially on her birthday!”

Poppy did a twirl.

"What a perfect Princess Poppy Party!"

FOR EMMA BROWN,
WHO WAS A TRUE PRINCESS

Published by Peppermint Press, 10B Kings Haugh, Edinburgh
First published 2003

Design & Print by Century 23, 17-19 Maritime Lane, Edinburgh.

ISBN 0-9546170 0-2